EMMa

EMMA
Emma Thompson

Usborne First Experiences

Going to school

Anne Civardi
Illustrated by Stephen Cartwright

Consultant: Betty Root

There is a little yellow duck hiding on every two pages. Can you find it?

The Peaches

MUM PEACH

DAD PEACH

POLLY PEACH

PONG

PING

PERCY PEACH

SIDNEY THE GERBIL

DUSTY

This is the Peach family. Percy and Polly are twins.
Tomorrow they are going to school for the first time.

The Peaches' flat

MILLIE MARSH

The Peaches live in a flat above the Marsh family. Millie Marsh is going to the same school as the twins.

Getting ready

At 8 o'clock, Mum and Dad wake Percy and Polly. It is time for them to get up and get dressed.

After breakfast, the twins put on their shoes and coats.
Millie is ready to go to school with them.

At school

MRS TODD

At first, Polly is a bit shy at school. Mrs. Todd, the teacher, says Mum can stay with her for a while.

Dad hangs Percy's coat on his own special hook. What has Percy brought with him to school?

In the classroom

There are a lot of things to do in the classroom, such as painting, drawing, reading and dressing up.

Some children make things out of paper, others make things with clay. What are Percy and Polly doing?

Making things

MR. JOLLY

MISS BERRY

Two of the teachers help the children make tiny washing lines full of clothes to take home.

Singing with Miss Dot

Miss Dot, the music teacher, teaches them to sing songs and to play all kinds of instruments.

Break time

At 11 o'clock, everyone has a drink and a biscuit. Percy and Polly are both very thirsty.

Story time

Mrs. Todd reads the children a story about a big tiger called Stripes. What is Percy up to now?

In the play ground

Before they go home, the children go outside to play.
There are lots of toys in the playground.

Polly loves going down the slide. Percy likes to play in the sand. What has Millie found?

Going home

It is time to go home. The twins have had a happy day at school. They have made lots of new friends.

First published in 1985. This enlarged edition first published in 1992. Usborne Publishing Ltd, 83-85 Saffron Hill, London EC1N 8RT, England. © Usborne Publishing Ltd, 1992.